W9-BKD-305

A Kooties Club MYSTERY

Membership Card

Name

Nickname

School

Age

Permission is granted by the publisher to reproduce the Kooties Club Membership Card.

The Mystery
of the Missing Heart

by M. J. Cosson

Perfection Learning® CA

Cover and Inside Illustrations: Michael A. Aspengren

Text © 1999 Perfection Learning® Corporation.
All rights reserved. No part of this book may be used
or reproduced in any manner whatsoever without
written permission from the publisher.
Printed in the United States of America.

For information, contact
Perfection Learning® Corporation,
1000 North Second Avenue, P.O. Box 500,
Logan, Iowa 51546-1099.
Phone: 1-800-831-4190 • Fax: 1-712-644-2392
Paperback 0-7891-2876-4
Cover Craft® 0-7807-7839-1
6 7 8 9 10 PP 09 08 07 06 05

Table of Contents

Introduction

Abe, Ben, Gabe, Toby, and Ty live in a large city. There isn't much for kids to do. There isn't even a park close by.

Their neighborhood is made up of apartment houses and trailer parks. Gas stations and small shops stand where the parks and grass used to be. And there aren't many houses with big yards.

Ty and Abe live in an apartment complex. Next door is a large vacant lot. It is full of brush, weeds, and trash. A path runs across the lot. On the other side is a trailer park. Ben and Toby live there.

Across the street from the trailer park is a big gray house. Gabe lives in the top apartment of the house.

The five boys have known each other since they started school. But they haven't always been friends.

The other kids say the boys have cooties. And the other kids won't touch them with a ten-foot pole. So Abe, Ben, Gabe, Toby, and Ty have formed their own club. They call it the Kooties Club.

Here's how to join. If no one else will have anything to do with you, you're in.

The boys call themselves the Koots for short. Ben's grandma calls his grandpa an *old coot.* And Ben thinks his grandpa is pretty cool. So if he's an old coot, Ben and his friends must be young koots.

The Koots play ball and hang out with each other. But most of all, they look for mysteries to solve.

Chapter 1

Lola Lockheart

"La-la, la-la, la-la!" Lola Lockheart sang.

Her fingers flew over the guitar strings. They flew as fast as hummingbird wings. Gabe tried to see how she did it.

"La-la, la-la, la-la!" she finished the song. She bowed low. Then she raised her arms high in the air and shook them.

The crowd went crazy. The people clapped and clapped.

Gabe sat in the front row. Several seats away sat Pam. They clapped along with everyone else.

"OK!" said Lola Lockheart. "One more song."

She sat down again. She began to play. This song was slow and sad.

Gabe watched her fingers move over the strings. He made up his mind. He would learn to play the guitar.

Lola Lockheart was famous. She made CDs and tapes. She gave concerts. She'd even been in movies. She had come back to her hometown to play for the Fish Fry Fair.

Lola Lockheart wore red pants, a purple top, and a gold belt. Shiny red sandals showed off her purple toenails.

11

Purple fingernails strummed the guitar. Lola Lockheart's big gold earrings were set with red and purple stones. They swayed as she moved.

Red, purple, and gold rings flashed on her fingers. Her long black hair hung down her back.

Pam watched Lola Lockheart. She wanted to be just like her when she grew up. She wanted to be a star dressed in red, purple, and gold. Pam made a mental note. Long black hair, she added.

"Oh, my heart. Oh, my homeland," sang Lola Lockheart. Tears rolled down her cheeks. When she finished, the crowd clapped again.

People came up on the stage. Some shook her hands. They tried to hug her.

Gabe remembered the man. He had parked the man's car in his yard just a few hours ago. Gabe thought the man looked like a gorilla.

Lola Lockheart waved to the crowd. But she kept walking. Everyone clapped and clapped.

After she was gone, Gabe turned to leave. He was going to meet the other Koots by the root beer stand.

Pam turned at the same time. They bumped into each other.

"Watch where you're going, boy!" said Pam.

"Watch where you're going, girl!" Gabe shot back.

They both went "Humph!" and walked away.

13

Chapter 2

Money Matters

Gabe's house was just a block from the Fish Fry Fair. Gabe's landlord lived on the ground floor. She was very old. She had white hair and walked with a cane.

For the Fish Fry Fair, she had let Gabe park cars in the yard. The other Koots had helped him. They parked six cars in the tiny yard. Now they had $12.

Gabe, Ty, Abe, Ben, and Toby each ordered a root beer. Now they had $8.25 left. They walked around the fair, looking at things.

There was a fishing contest. The biggest fish would bring a prize. The prize was a new rod and reel.

The boys looked at the fishing rod. They looked at all the food stands. Nobody wanted to eat fish. They got hot dogs instead. Now they had $3.25 left.

Pam met her friend Jade under the sign that said Fish Fry Fair. Jade's mom had given her $2.00. Pam was broke. And they were both hungry.

The girls went across the street to Pam's house. They could eat there for free! They would return when Lola Lockheart sang again in one hour.

Chapter 3

The Missing Ring

Pam and Jade sat in the first row. Pam had told Jade all about Lola Lockheart. She wanted Jade to see the purple polish, the earrings, and the huge flashy rings.

Gabe, Abe, Ty, Toby, and Ben sat a few feet away. They ate their hot dogs and drank their root beer.

The girls looked at the Koots. Gabe smiled at Pam. He had hot dog in his mouth.

"Yuck!" cried Pam.

Gabe just smiled bigger.

"What's he doing here?" asked Jade.

"He was at the last show too," said Pam. "He watched Lola like a hawk. I think he wants to steal her rings. He couldn't take his eyes off her hands."

The girls looked at Gabe. He was still enjoying his hot dog. Mustard was running down his arm. He licked it off.

"Gross!" the girls yelled. They looked the other way.

Gabe just smiled more.

The crowd began to clap. Everyone was ready for the show.

Soon Lola Lockheart came back on stage. Now she wore a long black dress, a shiny silver belt, and huge silver earrings.

Her long black hair was pulled back in a braid. She looked classy in black and silver. Pam made more mental notes. Braid, she added.

The crowd clapped and clapped. Lola Lockheart held up her hands. Now she wore silver rings. At last the crowd became quiet.

"Thank you," said Lola Lockheart. "Before I begin, I have something to say. I lost a ring this afternoon. It's gold with a big ruby. The ruby is heart-shaped. It is worth a lot of money. It may have slipped off my finger during my show."

"If you find it, please return it. It was a gift from a very dear friend. I will give a big reward to the one who returns my ring today. If no one finds it, I will turn the matter over to the police."

A murmur ran through the crowd. The people hushed as Lola Lockheart began to play.

Pam looked at Jade. "We can help Lola Lockheart," she said.

Jade nodded. "And get a reward," she added.

Ben looked at the other Koots.

"A mystery!" said Toby.

"A reward!" said Ty. Everyone but Gabe couldn't wait for the singing to stop.

Chapter 4

The Suspects

Pam thought back to the afternoon. Lola Lockheart had worn many rings. But her hands moved so fast, it was hard to see them clearly.

The Koots looked at the small stage. It was two steps up from the ground. Park benches sat around it. A low wall stood behind. And behind the wall were the rides.

An RV was parked a few yards away. Lola Lockheart had gone into the RV after her afternoon show.

How could she lose a ring? Could someone have stolen it?

Pam looked around. She saw a few people who had been at the last show.

There were two ladies with sunburned arms and straw hats. There was a redheaded lady with dark glasses and a guide dog.

There was the couple with the almost matching T-shirts. His read "I live to fish." Hers read "I fish to live." No one looked like a thief.

Pam had also seen Gabe that afternoon. Gabe had watched Lola Lockheart's hands closely. Was he looking at her rings? Even so, Pam wondered aloud. "How would he get one?"

She looked at Gabe again. He was still watching Lola's hands. Was he going to try for a silver ring now?

Pam whispered to Jade, "Let's follow Gabe. He may be the guilty one."

"OK," said Jade. "Think what we could buy with the reward money!"

As Lola Lockheart played, Gabe looked around. He saw people who'd been at the last show. He looked at Pam. She had watched Lola Lockheart very closely.

Gabe wondered if Pam could have the heart ring. Maybe it slipped off when Lola shook her arms. Maybe Pam caught it.

"What if I had the reward money?" he asked himself. "I could take guitar lessons. Or maybe buy a guitar and teach myself."

Gabe decided to follow Pam when the show was over.

"My heart sings!" Lola Lockheart ended her last song. She bowed low. Just like at the afternoon show. Then she raised her arms high in the air and shook them.

The crowd went wild. The same gorilla man hopped up on stage. He got between Lola and the crowd.

Lola and the man walked back toward the RV. The crowd kept

24

clapping. Finally, Lola came back to the stage.

"One more song," she said. "But first, please remember to return my ring if you find it. Just knock on my door." She pointed to the RV.

Lola Lockheart looked so sad. Pam felt sorry for her. She promised herself that she would find the ring.

"Now, please join me in singing 'This Land Is Our Land,'" said Lola Lockheart. She strummed her guitar and sang. The crowd sang along.

After Lola Lockheart left the stage, people began to leave. Soon the stage and seats were empty, except for Pam, Jade, and the Koots.

Pam waited for Gabe and his friends to go. She began to look around for the ring. The Koots looked for the ring too.

They checked all around the stage. Ty walked to Lola Lockheart's RV and back. Ben looked at every inch of ground. Toby and Abe checked all the benches.

Gabe just sat, drinking his root beer. He watched Pam. She was crawling around, looking under the park benches. Pam looked up. She saw Gabe watching her.

"Get a life!" she barked.

Before Gabe could answer, Toby called his name.

"Come on, Gabe," he yelled. "Let's go on a ride. We have money left!"

Gabe looked up. The Koots were waiting for him.

"OK," he said.

After the Koots left, the girls followed.

Chapter 5

Could It Be Gabe?

"I know Gabe has the ring," said Pam. "He was acting strange. After the show, everyone looked for the ring. But Gabe just sat there."

"How will we find out if he has the ring?" asked Jade.

"We'll bump into him. He'll spill his root beer all over himself. Then we'll pretend to help him wipe himself off," answered Pam.

"Touch him?" asked Jade. "Gross!"

"We need to feel his pockets," said Pam. "Do you have a better idea?"

"Couldn't we just tell a police officer?" asked Jade.

"We don't know for sure that he has the ring," answered Pam. "And if he does, the police will just take it and give it to Lola Lockheart. Then we won't get to meet her."

"And we won't get the reward," added Jade. "OK, I'll bump. And you touch."

They followed the Koots. The boys stopped to watch the Ferris wheel.

Pam said to Jade, "Go, girl. It's now or never."

Jade rushed up to Gabe just as he tipped his root beer up to catch the last few drops. She bumped into him. But it was too late. There wasn't enough root beer left to even wet the

28

front of his shirt.

Pam started laughing. She laughed
so hard, she had to sit down. Gabe
looked at Jade. She turned red.

"Excuse me," she said.

"Watch where you're going," said
Gabe. He looked at Pam on the
ground.

"What's wrong with her?" he asked Jade.

Jade just turned and walked away, leaving Pam laughing on the ground.

Finally, Pam calmed down. She stood up and ran after Jade. The Koots just looked at each other.

"I have an idea," said Ben. "There might be a pickpocket here. Why doesn't somebody go on the Ferris wheel? See if we can see anything from up there. The rest of us can watch people from the ground."

"Good idea," said Ty.

"You go, Gabe," said Abe. "Since we got the money from your yard."

Gabe and Toby got tickets to the ride. They walked through the gate and got on the Ferris wheel.

Chapter 6

Could It Be Pam?

From the Ferris wheel, the boys could see the whole fair. Gabe spotted Pam and Jade. He could tell that Jade was mad at Pam. But by the time the ride stopped, the girls were walking arm-in-arm past the Ferris wheel.

Abe, Ty, and Ben waited at the gate.

"See anything?" asked Ty.

"Nope. Did you?" asked Toby.

The Koots all shook their heads.

"Let's follow Pam and Jade," Gabe said.

"Why?" asked Ben.

"I think they're acting funny," Gabe said. "Maybe they know something about the ring."

"Might as well," said Ben. "We don't have any other leads."

The boys followed the girls past the other rides. Pam turned around when they got to the bumper cars.

"I hope they get on this ride," she told Jade. "This ride will jiggle anything out of a pocket."

The Koots stopped when Pam and Jade stopped. The boys didn't seem to be going on another ride.

"I think they're following us," said Jade.

"Why would they do that?" asked
Pam.

"To bug us," answered Jade.

"Let's duck in here," said Pam.
"We'll lose them. Then we'll turn the
tables and follow them. Just like we
planned."

The girls ducked between the Love
Bug and the merry-go-round. They
ran behind a trailer that was parked
behind the rides. A sign on the side of
the trailer said *Milo's Carnival, Tampa,
Florida.* Then they crawled under the
trailer.

The Koots saw the girls duck
between the two rides. But then they
lost them. The Koots walked around
the trailer with the sign *Milo's
Carnival, Tampa, Florida.* The girls
weren't there.

33

"They must be near," said Gabe. "Let's crawl under here. Maybe we'll see their feet when they walk by." The Koots crawled under the trailer.

Chapter 7

Surprises

The Koots crawled under the trailer. Toby, Ben, and Ty went first. Abe and Gabe followed them.

Toby bumped into something. It felt like a body. Before he could yell, the body went, "Eek!"

It was dark under the trailer. At first Toby couldn't see what he'd bumped into. Then he saw. It was Jade.

The two stared at each other. Slowly, the Koots' eyes got used to the dark. Then they saw that they were under the trailer with Pam and Jade.

Before anyone had a chance to speak, the trailer door opened. Someone stepped out. A pair of men's shoes was just a few feet from their faces.

A gruff male voice said, "Get this stuff to the car. I'll meet you in an hour. I want to be out of here tonight.

"She won't call the cops about the ring until tomorrow," the voice laughed. "We'll be out of the state by then."

The faces under the trailer looked surprised.

A voice inside the trailer said, "OK, pookums."

The door banged shut. The shoes began to walk way. The kids all inched to the edge of the trailer. Carefully, they peeked out.

The man they saw walking away was the gorilla man. He even walked like a gorilla. His long arms were swinging.

Gabe and Pam looked at each other. Their eyes wide.

"Now what'll we do?" whispered Pam.

"We have to get the ring from inside this trailer," whispered Gabe.

"We'll get killed," whispered Abe.

"We have to tell the police," whispered Jade.

"And we have to tell them fast. Before they take the ring away," whispered Ben.

"We have to tell Lola Lockheart," whispered Gabe.

Everybody agreed with him.

Just then, the door of the trailer opened again. Out came another pair of shoes. And four dog feet. All seven kids watched the six feet walk away.

"It's the redheaded lady with the guide dog!" exclaimed Pam. "She was at both concerts!"

Chapter 8

The Ring

"I bet she has the ring in her handbag," said Gabe.

"Let's just see if she left it inside. Maybe the door is unlocked," said Ty.

They all crawled from under the trailer. Gabe and Pam reached for the door at the same time. They turned the handle. The door was locked.

"We have to follow that lady," said Gabe.

Ben had already set out after her. The other kids caught up to him. The woman and her dog wove through the crowd. The kids hurried after her.

Suddenly the woman stopped. She bought a large lemonade. Something seemed fishy. When she got her change back, she looked at it.

Then she walked toward the sign that said *Fish Fry Fair.* Once she passed under the sign, she would be gone. The kids had to act fast.

Pam and Jade looked at each other. They nodded and winked.

"I'll bump," said Jade. She ran ahead. She shut her eyes and kept on running. She ran right into the red-headed lady.

The lemonade spilled all over her. The lady's sunglasses fell off. She looked right at Jade.

Her dog lay down. He was a very old dog. He seemed glad to have a chance to rest.

Pam, Gabe, Ben, Abe, Toby, and Ty were there to help.

"Oh, I'm sorry," said Jade. "Here, let me help you." She pulled a tissue from a pocket.

"Oh, let me help too," said Pam. She blotted the woman's dress with her sleeve.

"What's going on here?" she asked. "I can take care of myself. You kids get away!"

The redheaded lady started to back away from the kids. She fell over Toby, who had stooped to tie a shoe.

She landed flat on her back. Her handbag flew open. Its contents spilled all over the ground. There were watches, wallets, rings, and other loot.

The kids picked up the handbag and its contents.

"Let me help you up, ma'am," said Ben. He leaned over and gave the lady a hand. She stood up and brushed herself off. Her dog just sat and watched. Toby handed her handbag to her.

"Humph!" she said. She took her handbag and walked toward the Fish Fry Fair sign. Her dog followed.

As soon as the lady was out of sight, Abe held out his hand. He held a large, heart-shaped, gold and ruby ring.

"Is this it?" he asked.

"Yes!" shouted Pam.

"Let's run for it!" said Ben. He knew the woman would be checking her handbag.

All seven kids ran for Lola Lockheart's RV. They wove through the crowd.

The redheaded woman **had** checked her handbag. And she wasn't far behind them.

Chapter 9

The Getaway

Gabe pounded wildly on the RV door.

"Please let Lola Lockheart open the door," Pam pleaded quietly.

If the gorilla man opened the door, they were in big trouble. The kids all wished that they had stopped a police officer and asked for help. But there just hadn't been time. And now it was too late.

Knock! Knock! Knock! Gabe pounded again. Then Pam pounded too.

The door opened. A gray-haired lady peered out.

"Yes?" said the lady. "What do you want?"

Pam gulped. "We need to see Lola Lockheart," she said.

"What about?" asked the gray-haired lady. Her blue eyes looked cold. She frowned.

"About the ring," Pam whispered.

The lady looked slowly from Pam to Gabe to Jade to Ty to Abe. Finally she looked from Ben to Toby. It seemed to take forever before she spoke again.

Her eyes narrowed. "Do you have the ring?" she asked.

They all nodded.

47

"Come in," said the gray-haired lady.

Gabe, Pam, Abe, Ty, Toby, Ben, and Jade all took a deep breath. They walked into the RV just as the redheaded lady got there.

The gray-haired lady turned back to the door. "Yes?" she said to the red-headed lady.

"I'll wait for my kids out here," said the out-of-breath woman. She stood back a few feet. She looked like a parent on trick-or-treat night. Her dog sat beside her.

Inside, Lola Lockheart sat at a table. Across from her sat the gorilla man. They were eating dinner.

"These children have your ring, dear," said the gray-haired lady. Lola Lockheart jumped up in surprise.

"Oh, how wonderful!" she cried. She held out her hand. Abe placed the ring in it.

The gorilla man glared at the kids.

"Excuse me," he said. He walked out the trailer door. Ben looked out a window. He saw the gorilla man and the redheaded lady talking. Then they walked quickly away.

"Where did you find my ring?" asked Lola Lockheart. The kids quickly explained.

"Just a minute," said Lola Lockheart. She picked up a phone and dialed 911.

Lola Lockheart spoke softly into the phone. "Police. Yes. I need to report a crime."

49

Chapter 10

The Reward

As the Koots, Pam, and Jade left the Fish Fry Fair, they thought about what had happened.

The police had come. They had taken Lola Lockheart's report. The gorilla man was a con artist. He'd told her the Fish Fry Fair people had sent him to act as her bodyguard. **He** had stolen her ring.

The redheaded woman was his wife. She worked for the carnival that was part of the Fish Fry Fair.

The two had stolen things from many people at the fair. The trailer belonged to the carnival. But the man and woman had used it as a place to pool their loot.

When she wasn't working, the woman put on dark glasses and took her dog for a walk. She bumped into people. She picked their pockets or handbags. She would be long gone before anyone missed their things.

The police picked up the man and woman right away. They found them waiting in Gabe's yard.

To make more money, the Koots had packed too many cars into the small yard. The couple's car was blocked in. They couldn't drive away.

The gorilla man and the redheaded lady were at the police station now. They would spend the night in jail and maybe much longer.

"I wonder where the dog is," said Pam.

"I asked," said Ben. "A man at the carnival has it. He will keep it."

The kids were quiet, thinking about their new things. Instead of a money reward, Lola Lockheart had asked each kid what he or she wanted most.

Pam had said, "I want to be just like you."

Jade had said, "I want to be like you too."

The Koots didn't say anything.

"Oh, you must want something," said Lola Lockheart.

"Do you have bikes?" she asked. They all shook their heads no.

"Would you like a bike?" She looked at each kid. The Koots, Pam, and Jade nodded and smiled. All except Gabe.

"OK, then," she said. "Everyone gets a new bike."

Lola looked at Gabe. "I saw you watching me play the guitar. You want to play the guitar, don't you?"

"More than anything," said Gabe.

"Would you rather have a guitar?" asked Lola.

Gabe nodded.

"I'll be here all week," Lola said. "I'm visiting my mother." She pointed to the gray-haired lady.

"If you want to come by each day after school, I'll give you a lesson, Gabe."

53

Gabe's eyes got big. His face got red. "Sure!" he said.

"OK," said Lola. "Tomorrow we'll go shopping for bikes and a guitar. And after that, Gabe, you'll get your first lesson."

The kids all thanked Lola and left to walk home. They passed under the Fish Fry Fair sign.

"Another mystery solved by the great Kooties Club!" Gabe yelled. He and the Koots all did the Kootie handshake.

"If it hadn't been for us, Lola Lockheart's ring would be on its way out of the state by now," said Jade.

The Koots all looked at each other. Ty stepped forward.

"Thanks for helping us solve this mystery," he said.

"Humph!" said Jade.

"Humph!" said Pam.

They locked arms and walked off.

The Koots laughed and shook hands again.